MELLYBEAN AND THE VILLAINS' REVENGE

MIKE WHITE

RAZORBILL

An imprint of Penguin Random House LLC, New York

First published in the United States of America by Razorbill,
an imprint of Penguin Random House LLC, 2022

Visit us online at penguinrandomhouse.com.

Library of Congress Cataloging-in-Publication Data is available.

Manufactured in China

9780593202845 (hardcover); 9780593202869 (paperback)

1 3 5 7 9 10 8 6 4 2

TOPL

Design by Mike White
Colors by Valery Kutz
Text set in Evil Genius

Dedicated to
Jeff, Nurgul, Wolfie, Jared, and Wall-E

With special thanks to my family, the Hou family, the Kim family, and the Keeler family for their love and support

CHAPTER 1
GUESS WHO'S BACK

HELP! HELP! CAN ANYBODY HEAR ME?!

ARRRRGH!

MY LORD! THERE YOU ARE!

I HAVEN'T STOPPED LOOKING FOR YOU SINCE THE DAY OF THE RACE.

I'M SO GLAD YOU'RE OKAY AND--

PLUNK!

IT'S ABOUT TIME YOU FOUND ME! WHAT TOOK YOU SO LONG?!
...AND LIKE YOUR OLD SELF.

GURGLE!

QUIET, YOU!

HERE, I BROUGHT YOU SOME BREAD IN CASE YOU MIGHT BE--
FOOD!

NOM
NOM
NOM
NOM

NOM
NOM
NOM
NOM
...HUNGRY.

AND NOT TO WORRY, MY LORD, I HAVE A PLAN TO GET THE KINGDOM BACK.
THAT SCRUFFY PUP GAVE THE CROWN TO THE GIANT MONSTER, BUT THINGS ARE ALREADY IN THE WORKS TO GET BACK WHAT'S RIGHTFULLY YOURS.

GOOD, GOOD. NOW GET ME OUT OF HERE.

UH...

YOU *DO* KNOW THE WAY OUT, RIGHT?

OF COURSE! IT'S THIS WAY...

I THINK...

HOURS LATER...
THERE IT IS! THE WAY OUT!

GAH! IT'S TOO BRIGHT OUT HERE!

SORRY, MY LORD. HERE, HAVE SOME SHADE.

AHHH...
THAT'S BETTER.

SO, HOW ABOUT YOU TELL ME ABOUT THIS PLAN OF YOURS TO GET ME MY CROWN BACK?

CHAPTER 2
KEEP-AWAY

YOUR FOOD STARE ONLY WORKS ON THE HUMANS, MELLYBEAN.

BESIDES, YOU KNOW YOU'RE NOT ALLOWED TO EAT CAT FOOD.

WHIMPER

HAVE YOU NOTICED THAT I HAVEN'T BARKED AT YOU FOR EATING WIRES, SCRATCHING THE SOFA, OR BEING ON THE COUNTER?

THAT'S BECAUSE EVERYTHING HERE IS MADE OF WOOD AND STONE...THERE ARE NO WIRES OR SOFAS!

BUT YOU NOTICED, RIGHT? I'M BEING EXTRA NICE. THAT MEANS YOU SHOULD SHARE YOUR FOOD WITH ME.

NOT A CHANCE, MELLY.

AW...

HEY, DON'T PLAY WITH THAT--IT'S OUR LAST CAN UNTIL TUGS GETS BACK WITH ANOTHER HAUL!

SO, YOU WANT THIS?

YES. GIVE IT BACK, PLEASE.

OH BOY! A GAME OF KEEP-AWAY!

HEY! COME BACK HERE WITH THAT!

YEAH! BAD DOG!

WHEE! HA HA HA!

HA HA HA!

ERT!

UH-OH!

GOTCHA!

YOU'RE CORNERED, MELLYBEAN.
YOU'VE GOT NOWHERE TO RUN. TIME TO DROP IT.

NOW BACK AWAY FROM THE CAN...SLOWLY.

EASY...
EASY...

HETTY! CAN I GET A LITTLE HELP HERE?!

SURE THING!

HEY!

NO FAIR!

YEAH, THAT'S CHEATING!

HA HA HA!
NOW WE'LL GET
YOU, MELLYBEAN!

WHEE!
YOU CAN'T
CATCH ME!

COME BACK WITH
OUR FOOD!

BOF!

I REALLY GOTTA WORK ON MY LANDINGS.

ERT!

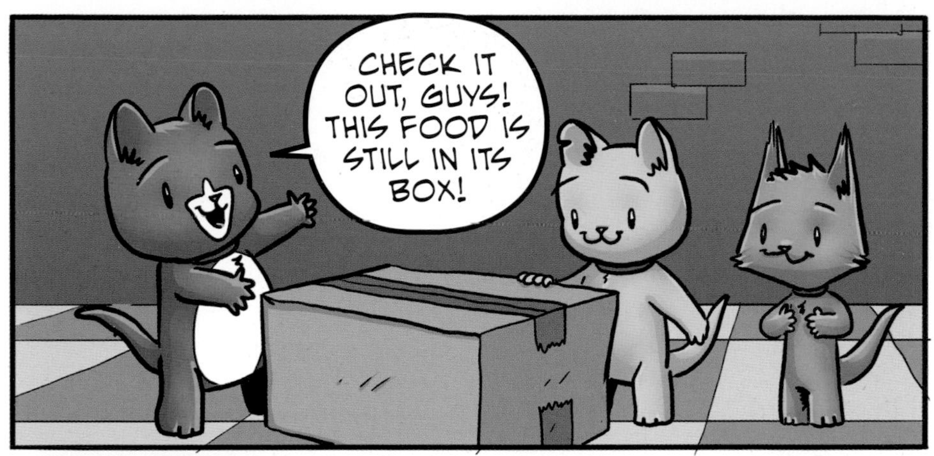
CHECK IT OUT, GUYS! THIS FOOD IS STILL IN ITS BOX!

MORE FOOD AND A BOX! OH BOY!

I CALL FIRST DIBS ON SITTING IN IT!

BUT WHAT ABOUT PLAYING KEEP-AWAY?

THIS IS A BETTER GAME, MELLY!
OH YEAH... THAT'S THE STUFF!

ME TOO, ME TOO!

ME THREE, ME THREE!

ISN'T THIS THE LIFE? I SURE COULD GO FOR A CAN OF SAVORY SALMON FEAST RIGHT NOW...

NOW, WHERE IS THE ROYAL CAN OPENER?

HEY, YEAH...
WHERE IS WILMA?

I HAVEN'T SEEN HER SINCE SHE OPENED THE LAST BATCH OF CANS WHEN THE CATS ARRIVED.

I WONDER WHERE SHE COULD BE.

OR WHAT SHE MIGHT BE UP TO...

CHAPTER 3
WEIRD SCIENCE
THERE WE GO!

WITHOUT MY MAGIC, I'LL HAVE TO RELY ON SCIENCE TO GET ME WHAT I WANT.

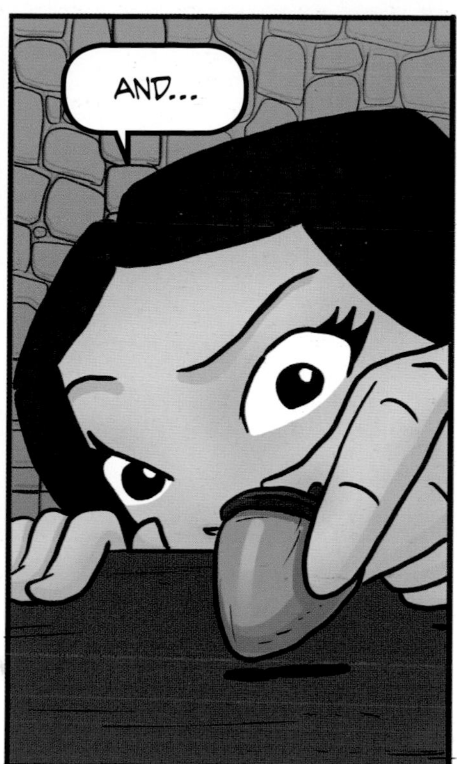
AND...

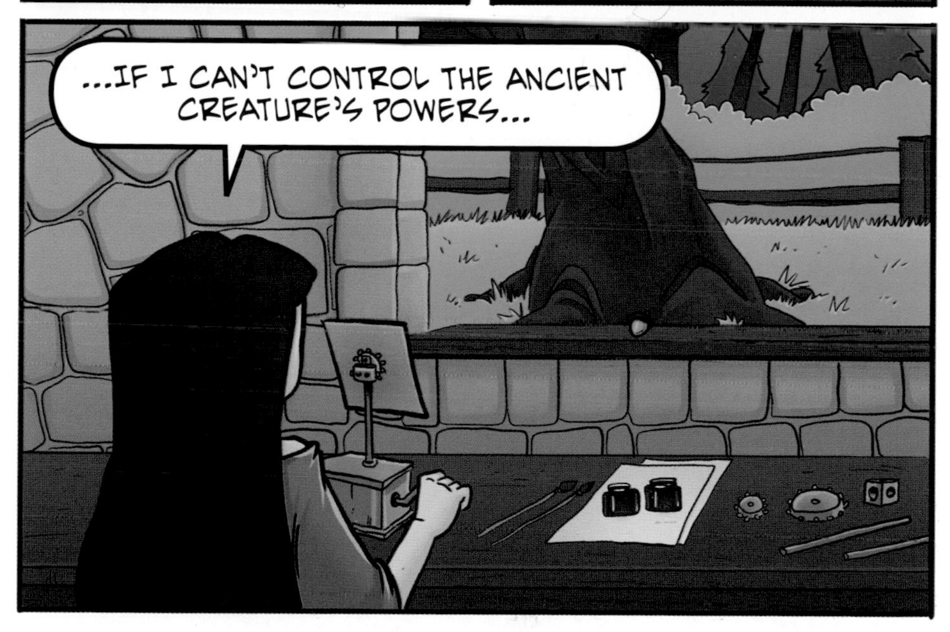
...IF I CAN'T CONTROL THE ANCIENT CREATURE'S POWERS...

SNIFF
SNIFF
SNIFF

...I'LL JUST HAVE TO CONTROL THE CREATURE!

I'LL BE TAKING THAT!

IT WORKS!
IT WORKS!
HA HA HA HA HA!

WE'RE HERE!

HELLO, WILMA!

FOOD!

NOM
NOM
NOM

AHHH! HOT!
HOT! HOT!

HOW IS YOUR INVENTION
COMING ALONG?

SEE FOR YOURSELF!
NOW I CAN CONTROL THE MIND OF ANY CREATURE I WANT!

HAVE YOU KEPT UP *YOUR* END OF THE BARGAIN?

WHY YES, YES I HAVE.

MY SPIES WERE ABLE TO FIND THE SECRET LAIR OF THE GRIFFINBEAR. THIS IS THE MAP.

GRIFFINBEAR?! DON'T TELL ME YOU'RE GOING AFTER THAT HULKING BRUTE WITHOUT AN ARMY... SO MANY OF MY SOLDIERS NEVER CAME BACK FROM HUNTING HIM!

OH, DEAR KING, YOU UNDERESTIMATE MY ABILITY TO OUTWIT HUMANS AND CREATURES ALIKE.

WITH MY MACHINE, I WILL BRAINWASH THE GRIFFINBEAR. THEN THE REST OF THEM WILL FALL IN LINE OUT OF FEAR BECAUSE I WILL HAVE THE MOST POWERFUL ANCIENT CREATURE UNDER MY CONTROL!

AND ONCE I HAVE ALL OF THEIR POWERS AT MY COMMAND, YOU CAN HAVE YOUR PRECIOUS CROWN!

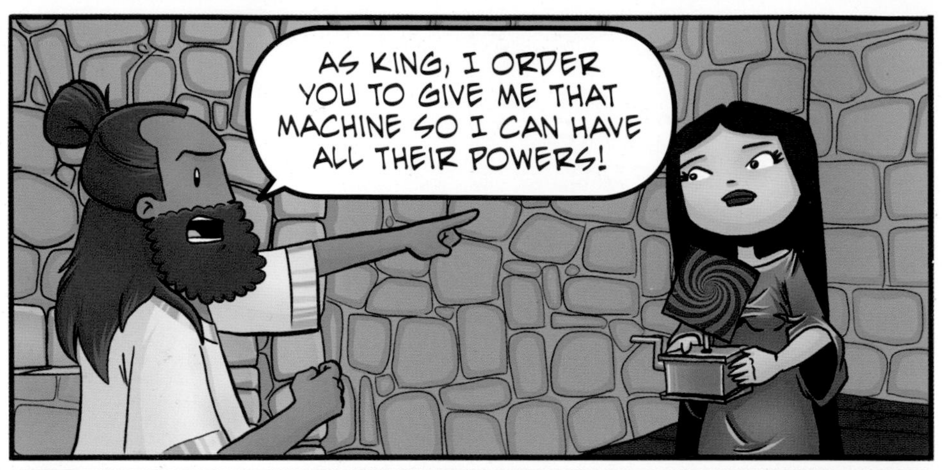
AS KING, I ORDER YOU TO GIVE ME THAT MACHINE SO I CAN HAVE ALL THEIR POWERS!

THAT WASN'T OUR AGREEMENT!

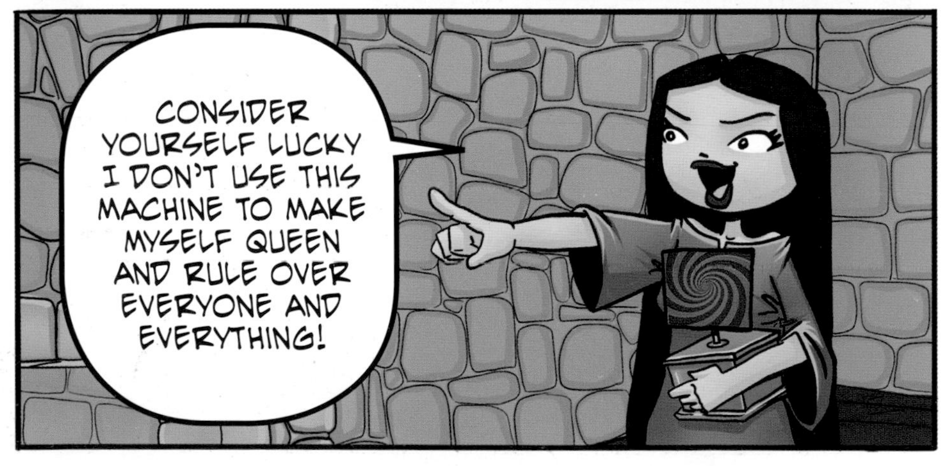
CONSIDER YOURSELF LUCKY I DON'T USE THIS MACHINE TO MAKE MYSELF QUEEN AND RULE OVER EVERYONE AND EVERYTHING!

HEY NOW... YOU SAID THAT IF I GOT YOU A MAP TO THE GRIFFINBEAR, YOU COULD GET US THE CROWN. THAT IS A FAIR TRADE.

AW, NUTS.

FINE. FINE. A DEAL'S A DEAL. YOU CAN HAVE THE CROWN, BUT ONLY IF THIS MAP PROVES TO BE RELIABLE.
NOW GET YOUR CLOAKS SO WE CAN GO GRIFFINBEAR-HUNTING!

CHAPTER 4
WAY BACK WHEN

NOT NOW, MELLY. WE'RE DOING IMPORTANT STUFF HERE--MY TURN AGAIN, MY TURN AGAIN!

CHECK OUT **THIS** SIT.

OOOOHHH... NICE ONE!

WHAT ARE YOU GUYS UP TO?

DO EITHER OF YOU WANT TO CHASE ME?

WE WERE JUST TALKING ABOUT THE GOOD OLD DAYS...
WHEN ALL FOUR OF US ANCIENT CREATURES WERE LAST TOGETHER HUNDREDS OF YEARS AGO.

REALLY? WHAT WAS IT LIKE BACK THEN?

MORE MAGICAL! BEING ABLE TO CONTROL AIR, WATER, EARTH, AND LIFE, THE FOUR OF US COULD BASICALLY SHAPE THE LAND OF ADO ANY WAY YOU CAN IMAGINE.

SO WHAT HAPPENED? WHERE DID THE OTHERS GO?

NOBODY KNOWS...
WHEN I FIRST BEFRIENDED WILMA, LEMMY, THE GRIFFINBEAR, AND RETTA, THE DRAGONSEAL, WERE SUSPICIOUS OF OUR FRIENDSHIP.
THEY DIDN'T LIKE HER PESTERING ME TO SHARE OUR SECRETS. SHE KEPT WANTING TO KNOW ABOUT EACH OF US ANCIENT CREATURES AND OUR POWERS.

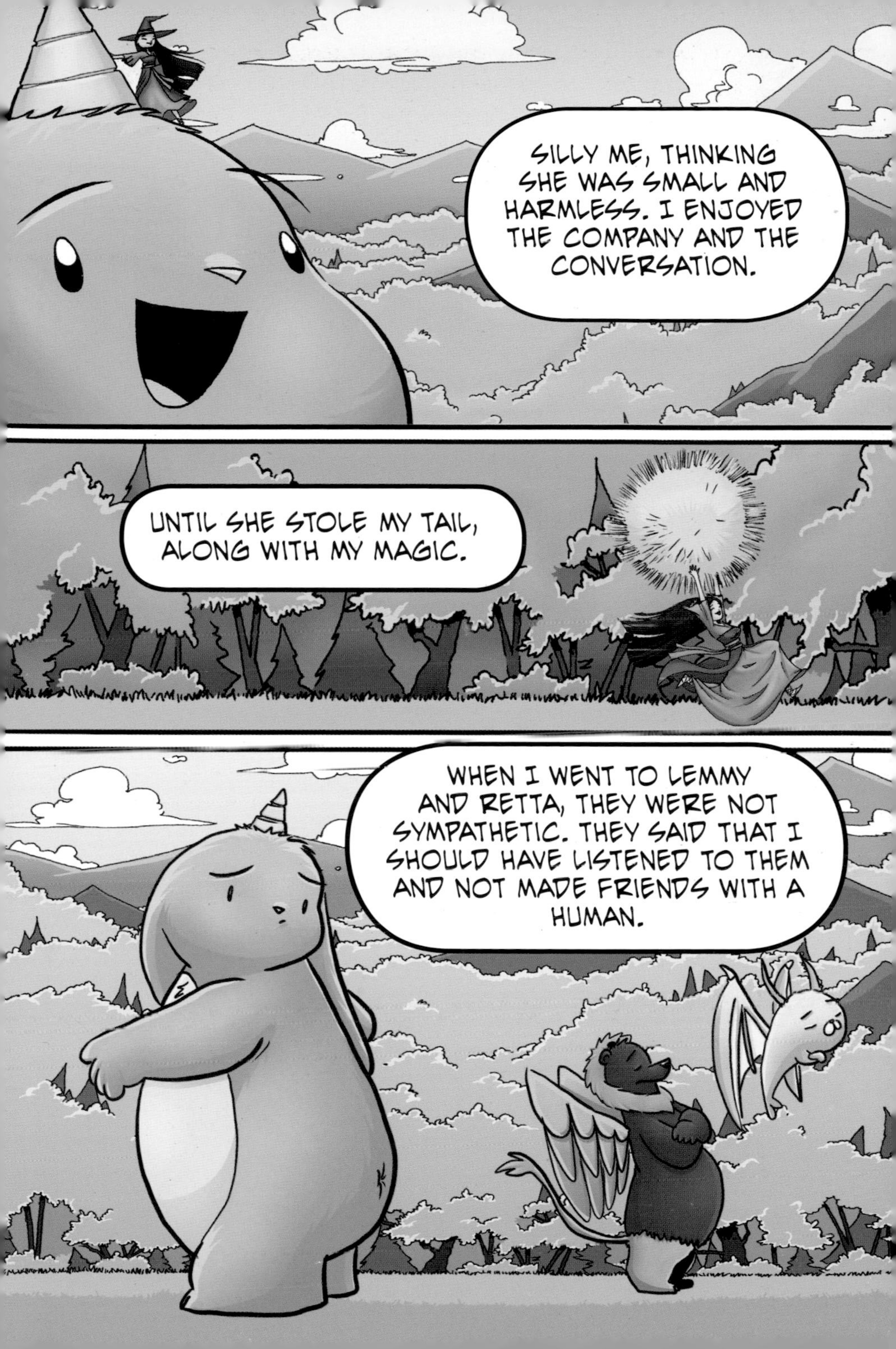
SILLY ME, THINKING SHE WAS SMALL AND HARMLESS. I ENJOYED THE COMPANY AND THE CONVERSATION.
UNTIL SHE STOLE MY TAIL, ALONG WITH MY MAGIC.
WHEN I WENT TO LEMMY AND RETTA, THEY WERE NOT SYMPATHETIC. THEY SAID THAT I SHOULD HAVE LISTENED TO THEM AND NOT MADE FRIENDS WITH A HUMAN.

FEARING THAT THE HUMANS WOULD TAKE AWAY THEIR POWERS, LIKE WILMA DID TO ME, LEMMY AND RETTA DECIDED TO GO INTO HIDING.
HETTY STAYED WITH ME FOR A WHILE...
...UNTIL THE SOLDIERS STARTED COMING AROUND AND SHE FLED FOR HER SAFETY.

THE KING AT THE TIME--
THE GREAT-GREAT-GREAT...

...GREAT-GREAT-GREAT-GRANDFATHER OF THE KING YOU RACED...
STARTED HUNTING ALL CREATURES, THINKING THAT THEY HAD POWERS TOO, AND NOT JUST US FOUR.

AND THAT'S WHY THEY'VE BEEN HIDING ALL THESE YEARS.

SO IT WAS THE GREEDINESS OF WILMA AND THE KINGS THAT DROVE ALL OF THE CREATURES AWAY?

YEAH. FOR GENERATIONS, KINGS HAVE SENT THEIR ARMIES TO HUNT US, NEVER GIVING UP!

BUT AFTER YOU CAME ALONG AND MADE NARRA THE KING, WE STARTED TO FEEL SAFE AGAIN, AND WE CAME OUT OF HIDING! WELL, MOST OF US.

LEMMY AND RETTA MUST STILL BE SUSPICIOUS OF HUMANS TRYING TO ATTACK THEM AND TAKE THEIR POWERS.

WE SHOULD GO FIND THEM AND TELL THEM THAT WON'T HAPPEN ANYMORE! IT WILL BE JUST LIKE A GAME OF HIDE-AND-SEEK! I'M SURE THEY WILL BE SO GLAD TO SEE YOU AGAIN!

WILMA DID MENTION THAT THE DRAGONSEAL WAS LAST KNOWN TO BE SOMEWHERE IN THE NORTH SEA. MAYBE WE CAN TRY LOOKING THERE?

YAY! COME ON, GUYS, ANOTHER ADVENTURE AWAITS!

NAH, WE'RE GOOD. YOU GO AND HAVE FUN, THOUGH!

AW, COME ON--WE COULD USE YOUR HELP TO FIND NARRA AND HETTY'S FRIENDS!

HETTY, CAN YOU GIVE ME A HAND WITH THESE GUYS?

COMING RIGHT UP!

WHOA, HEY!
WHAT'S GOING ON?

YAY! EVERYBODY, FOLLOW ME!

UH, MELLY?

NORTH IS *THAT* WAY.
OH.

TEE-HEE. COME ON, EVERYBODY, *THIS* WAY!

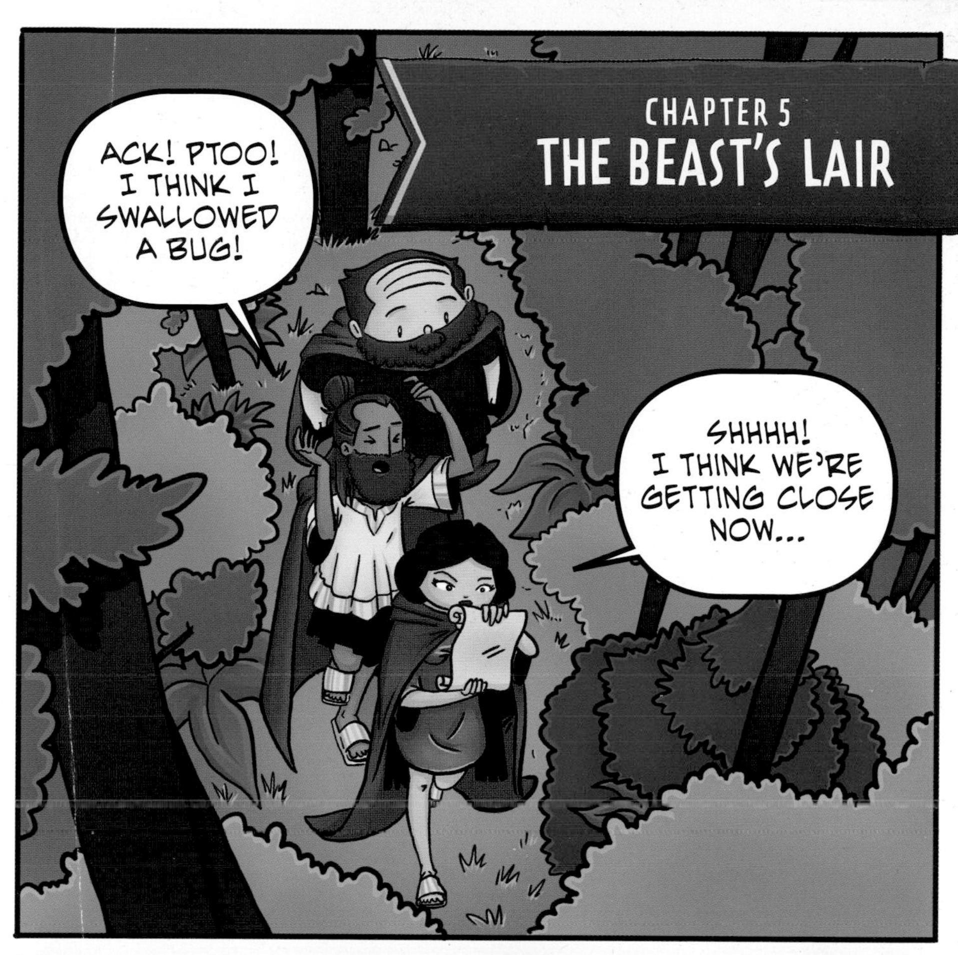
CHAPTER 5
THE BEAST'S LAIR
ACK! PTOO! I THINK I SWALLOWED A BUG!
SHHHH! I THINK WE'RE GETTING CLOSE NOW...

I THINK THIS IS IT!

THE MAP SAYS IT SHOULD BE RIGHT ABOUT HERE.

ONE OF YOU SHOULD GO AND CHECK IF HE'S IN THERE.

WHAT?! NO WAY!

WHY? ARE YOU SCARED? DON'T YOU WANT THE CROWN ANYMORE?

YE--NO!
I'M NOT SCARED TECHNICALLY, JUST, UM...

RAWR!
EEEK!

SHOOP!

HA HA HA
HA HA!

YOU'RE SCARED OF THE BIG, MEAN, OLD GRIFFINBEAR!
HEE-HEE, RAWR!

WHO DARES DISTURB MY SLUMBER?!

SHOOP!

IT SOUNDS AS IF THERE ARE HUMANS AT MY DOOR!

UH, UH...YES, THREE NICE HUMANS WHO HAVE A PRESENT FOR YOU IF YOU'D CARE TO COME OUT.

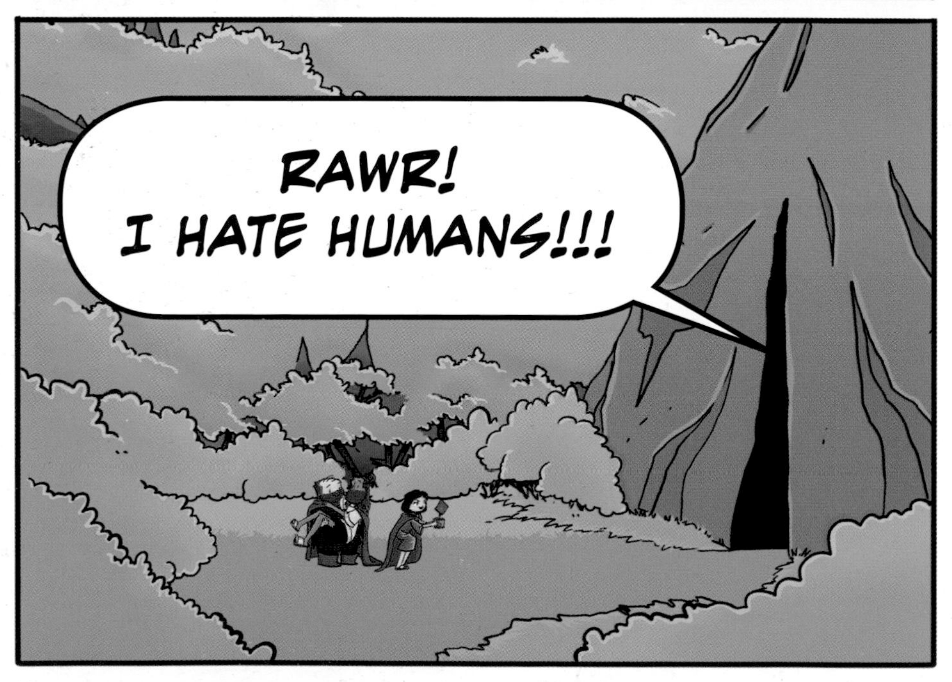
RAWR! I HATE HUMANS!!!

NOW, WHICH ONE OF YOU WANTS TO BE MY BREAKFAST?!

RAWR!!!

LET'S GET OUT OF HERE!

TEE-HEE, UM...

HERE'S YOUR PRESENT...

HMMM...WHAT IS THIS THING SUPPOSED TO BE?

JUST KEEP LOOKING AT IT. YOU'LL SEE...

HA HA HA HA!

BOW DOWN TO ME.

YOUR WISH IS MY COMMAND.

MWA HA HA
HA HA!

WOW, IT WORKED!
I TOTALLY THOUGHT SHE WAS GOING TO GET EATEN.

PICK UP THOSE TWO SO WE CAN CONTINUE OUR JOURNEY!

AAAAAAAHHHH!

NOW LET'S FLY NORTH TO FIND THE DRAGONSEAL!

AS YOU COMMAND.

CHAPTER 6
THE NORTH SEA

LET'S SET DOWN OVER THERE ON THE SHORE AND TAKE A LOOK AROUND.

OH BOY! I LOVE THE BEACH AND ALL THE GREAT SMELLS!

DON'T YOU GUYS LOVE THE BEACH TOO?

YEAH! IT'S LIKE WE'RE IN A GIANT LITTER BOX!

LOOK AT ALL THIS FRESH SAND JUST WAITING FOR US TO POOP IN IT!

THERE'S NOTHING BETTER THAN A CLEAN BATHROOM.

EXCEPT MAYBE THIS BOX. THIS BOX IS PRETTY GREAT.

HEY, CHECK IT OUT. IF YOU TURN THE BOX ON ITS SIDE, IT'S JUST LIKE HAVING A ROOM ON THE BEACH!

OUR OWN LITTLE BEACH ROOM... PRETTY SWEET.

BATH-ROOM...

BEACH ROOM...

BATH-ROOM.

BEACH ROOM!
THIS IS SO GLAMOROUS!

THERE THEY GO WITH THE BOX AGAIN. THEY'RE **OBSESSED!**

HOW CAN I GET THEM TO SNAP OUT OF IT?

MAYBE A SPLASH OF COLD WATER WILL DO THE TRICK!

SPLOOSH!

HEY!
ACK!
PBPBPBTH!

OKAY, OKAY, WE'LL STOP PLAYING WITH THE BOX.
WHAT IS IT YOU WANT US TO DO?

WOW, GOOD THINKING, NARRA. HOW DID YOU KNOW THAT WOULD WORK?

INTUITION! A NICE SPLASH OF COLD WATER ALWAYS HELPS ME CLEAR MY HEAD.

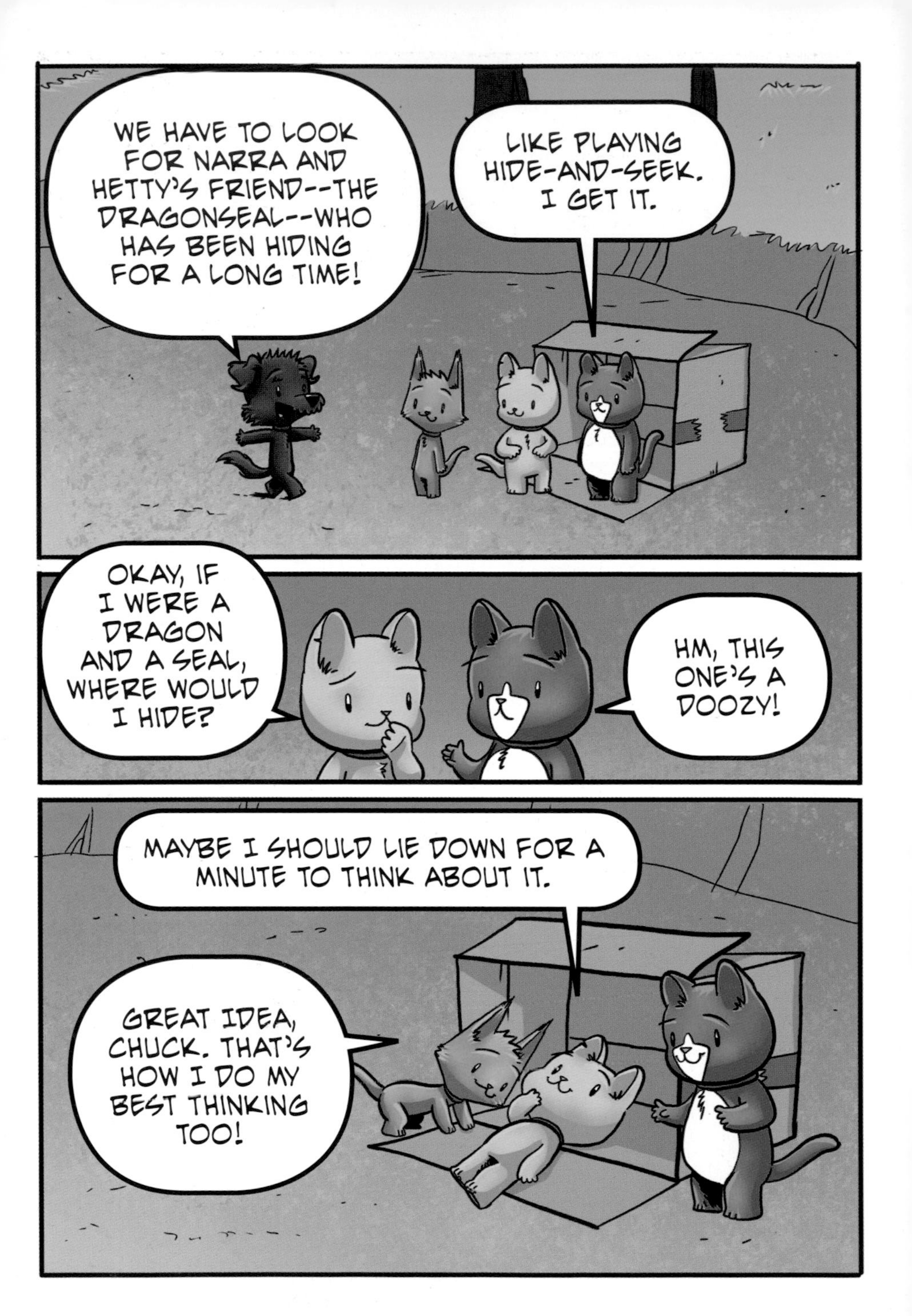
WE HAVE TO LOOK FOR NARRA AND HETTY'S FRIEND--THE DRAGONSEAL--WHO HAS BEEN HIDING FOR A LONG TIME!
LIKE PLAYING HIDE-AND-SEEK. I GET IT.
OKAY, IF I WERE A DRAGON AND A SEAL, WHERE WOULD I HIDE?
HM, THIS ONE'S A DOOZY!
MAYBE I SHOULD LIE DOWN FOR A MINUTE TO THINK ABOUT IT.
GREAT IDEA, CHUCK. THAT'S HOW I DO MY BEST THINKING TOO!

YOU'RE DEFINITELY ONTO SOMETHING HERE.

GUYS! YOU'RE BACK IN THE BOX AGAIN!

YOU'RE SUPPOSED TO BE HELPING. THIS LOOKS LIKE NAPPING!
WE'RE THINKING.
YEAH, WE'RE--

RUMBLE

CRA-
CRACK!

WHOA!
AAAAAAAAAAAAAA!
CRUMBLE

CRACK!

DON'T WORRY, I GOT YOU!
CRA-CRACK!
SWOOSH!

THE GROUND IS TAKING HOLD OF NARRA'S FEET!

IT'S SOME KIND OF MAGIC! THIS CAN ONLY BE THE WORK OF--

THE GRIFFINBEAR!

LEMMY!
WHAT ARE YOU
DOING WITH
WILMA?

SHE HAS HIM UNDER A SPELL!

HOW DID YOU GET YOUR POWERS BACK, WILMA?

NO MAGIC TRICKS THIS TIME, NARRA. JUST GOOD OLD-FASHIONED SCIENCE!

WHAT IS THAT?
I CAN'T TELL...

JUST WAIT, YOU'LL SEE!

UH-OH, SOMETHING IS HAPPENING...

EEP!

AAAAAAAAAAAAA!
WHOA!
SPLOOSH!
SPLOOSH!

LOOK, WILMA HAS DONE SOMETHING TO NARRA AND HETTY!

THEY ARE UNDER MY MIND CONTROL, LITTLE SCRUFFY DOG!

NOW RETURN THE CROWN TO THE KING!

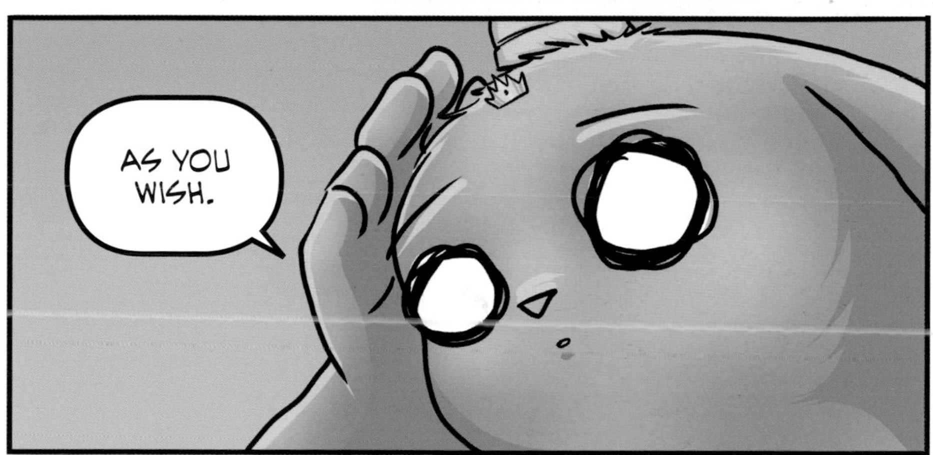
AS YOU WISH.

HA HA HA HA HA HA HA!

I SHALL BE RULER OF HUMANKIND ONCE AGAIN!

NOW THAT I AM KING AGAIN, I ORDER YOU TO GIVE ME THAT MACHINE!

NOT A CHANCE!

AW, BUT I'M THE KING AND YOU HAVE TO DO WHAT I SAY!

I ANSWER TO NO ONE! GRIFFINBEAR, TAKE HIS CROWN!

HEY!

THAT'S WHAT YOU GET FOR BEING GREEDY.

NOW I SHALL BE THE RULER OF BOTH HUMANS AND CREATURES!

YOU'LL NEVER GET AWAY WITH THIS, WILMA!

OH, TINY, SCRUFFY ONE, ANOTHER OUTBURST LIKE THAT AND I MIGHT JUST HYPNOTIZE YOU TOO!

NOW, BEGONE WITH YOU! HIPPOCORN, BLOW THEM OUT TO SEA!

AS YOU COMMAND, YOUR HIGHNESS.

HA HA! I JUST HAVE TO CATCH THE DRAGONSEAL, THEN MY PLAN WILL BE COMPLETE! I'LL HAVE CONTROL OF ALL THE WORLDLY POWERS!

GRIFFINBEAR, I THINK YOU CAN RELEASE NARRA NOW.

HIPPOCORN, BRING THE FORMER KING AND HIS ADVISER. THEY SHALL BE MY NEW SERVANTS!

CHAPTER 7
HOPELESSLY ADRIFT

AW, NO ONE'S GOING TO HEAR US ALL THE WAY OUT HERE. WE'RE DOOMED.

WE SHOULD BE OKAY FOR A WHILE AS LONG AS WE DON'T SPRING A LEAK.

FSSSSHHH!

OKAY, NOW WE'RE DOOMED.

QUICK, SCOOP OUT THE WATER!

KA- CHUNK!

HEY, DID ANYONE ELSE FEEL THAT? I THINK WE HIT SOMETHING!

OH NO, WHAT MORE CAN GO WRONG?

LAND!

OH BOY!

WE'VE WASHED UP ON A TINY ISLAND!

YOU'VE GOT THE "TINY" PART RIGHT.

WELL, AT LEAST WE'RE NOT SINKING ANYMORE.

TRUE. BUT I THINK OUR BOX HAS JUST ABOUT HAD IT.
OH NO!
GOODBYE, OLD FRIEND. YOU SERVED US WELL.

GLUB
GLUB
GLUB

UH...SORRY TO INTERRUPT, BUT HOW ARE WE GOING TO GET OFF THIS ISLAND?

HM. THAT'S A GOOD QUESTION. I THINK BARKING AND MEOWING UNTIL A HUMAN COMES MIGHT BE OUR ONLY OPTION.

WELL, OKAY THEN.

BARK! BARK! BARK!
MEOW!
MEOW!
MEOW!

RUMBLE

OH NO! WILMA MUST BE COMING BACK!

DO YOU MIND KEEPING IT DOWN? I'M TRYING TO SLEEP.

OH! WELL, HELLO THERE!

HI.

SORRY FOR ALL THE NOISE, BUT WE'RE KIND OF LOST AND--

YEAH, I'M NOT REALLY INTERESTED. I'D JUST LIKE TO GO BACK TO SLEEP, THANKS.

IT'S JUST THAT WILMA HYPNOTIZED OUR FRIENDS AND LEFT US OUT HERE AND--

WILMA! THE WIZARD? SHE'S NOT AROUND, IS SHE? SHE'S BAD NEWS. I'M OUTTA HERE.

GLUB
GLUB
GLUB

WAIT! WAIT!
NONE OF US CAN SWIM!

WILMA'S NOT A WIZARD ANYMORE!

NOW SHE'S GOT A HYPNOSIS MACHINE, AND SHE'S CAPTURED OUR FRIENDS.

AND WHEN SHE FINDS THE DRAGONSEAL, SHE'LL HAVE ALL THE POWERS TO CONTROL THE WORLD!

WHEW!
OH, THANK GOODNESS!

YOU DON'T SAY...

SHE'S LOOKING FOR THE DRAGONSEAL?

YES. AND SO WERE WE...
...THAT IS, UNTIL WILMA SHOWED UP WITH THE GRIFFINBEAR AND--

WHAT DO YOU KNOW OF THE GRIFFINBEAR?

WELL, NOT MUCH OTHER THAN THAT HE CONTROLS THE GROUND AND DOES WHATEVER WILMA SAYS...

HM. THAT DOESN'T SOUND LIKE LEMMY AT ALL.

WE'RE FRIENDS WITH NARRA AND HETTY. WE WERE GOING TO REUNITE THEM WITH THEIR OLD FRIENDS THE DRAGONSEAL AND THE GRIFFINBEAR, BUT WILMA CAME ALONG AND MESSED IT ALL UP!
FRIENDS OF NARRA AND HETTY, EH?

YEAH, I HELPED NARRA BECOME THE KING--

OH! THEN YOU MUST BE THE FAMOUS MELLYBEAN!

YEAH, THAT'S ME! NICE TO MEET YOU, UH...

THE NAME IS RETTA...

...RETTA, THE DRAGONSEAL!

CHAPTER 8
REUNITED
REALLY? IT'S YOU? OH BOY! NARRA AND HETTY WILL BE SO HAPPY, ONCE YOU HELP US FREE THEM!
I'LL DROP YOU OFF BACK ONSHORE, BUT I CAN'T HELP YOU WITH YOUR FIGHT.
WAIT, WHY NOT?

BECAUSE I'M NOT GETTING INVOLVED WITH ANY HUMAN TROUBLES. I LEARNED LONG AGO THAT THEY ARE NOT TO BE TRUSTED AND SHOULD BE AVOIDED AT ALL COSTS.

BUT WHAT ABOUT HELPING YOUR FRIENDS? WILMA IS CONTROLLING THEIR MINDS!

EXACTLY! ONE MORE REASON TO STAY AWAY! AND YOU SHOULD TOO, OR ELSE SHE MIGHT END UP CAPTURING ALL OF YOU!

COME ON, GUYS, BACK ME UP HERE. WE NEED TO SAVE OUR FRIENDS INSTEAD OF JUST HIDING AND IGNORING THE PROBLEM, RIGHT?

WELL, WHEN YOU FIRST FELL DOWN THE HOLE IN THE BACKYARD, WE JUST NAPPED...BUT THEN WE REALIZED THAT WE MIGHT GET IN TROUBLE, SO WE DECIDED TO GO AFTER YOU.

IS THERE SOME WAY THAT RETTA COULD GET IN TROUBLE IF SHE DOESN'T HELP?

GREAT THINKING!

RETTA, IF YOU DON'T HELP YOUR FRIENDS, WILMA WILL HAVE THE POWERS OF EARTH, AIR, AND LIFE...
YOU CAN'T LET HER BE IN CONTROL OF ALL THE ELEMENTS. THERE'S NO TELLING WHAT SHE WILL DO AND HOW IT MIGHT AFFECT THE WORLD.

AND ISN'T WILMA AFTER YOU TOO? SO SHE COULD USE THE POWERS OF THE OTHERS TO FIND YOU.

THAT WON'T BE NECESSARY!

NARRA, HETTY, LEMMY!

WHAT HAVE YOU DONE TO MY FRIENDS?!

SAME THING I'M GOING TO DO TO YOU!

HERE, I BROUGHT YOU A PRESENT!

DON'T LOOK! IT'S A TRAP! YOU'LL END UP LIKE THE OTHERS.

ARRRGGH! I WISH YOU'D STOP MEDDLING IN MY AFFAIRS, TINY DOG!

BUNNYCORN, HIPPOCORN, GRIFFINBEAR, GET THEM!!!

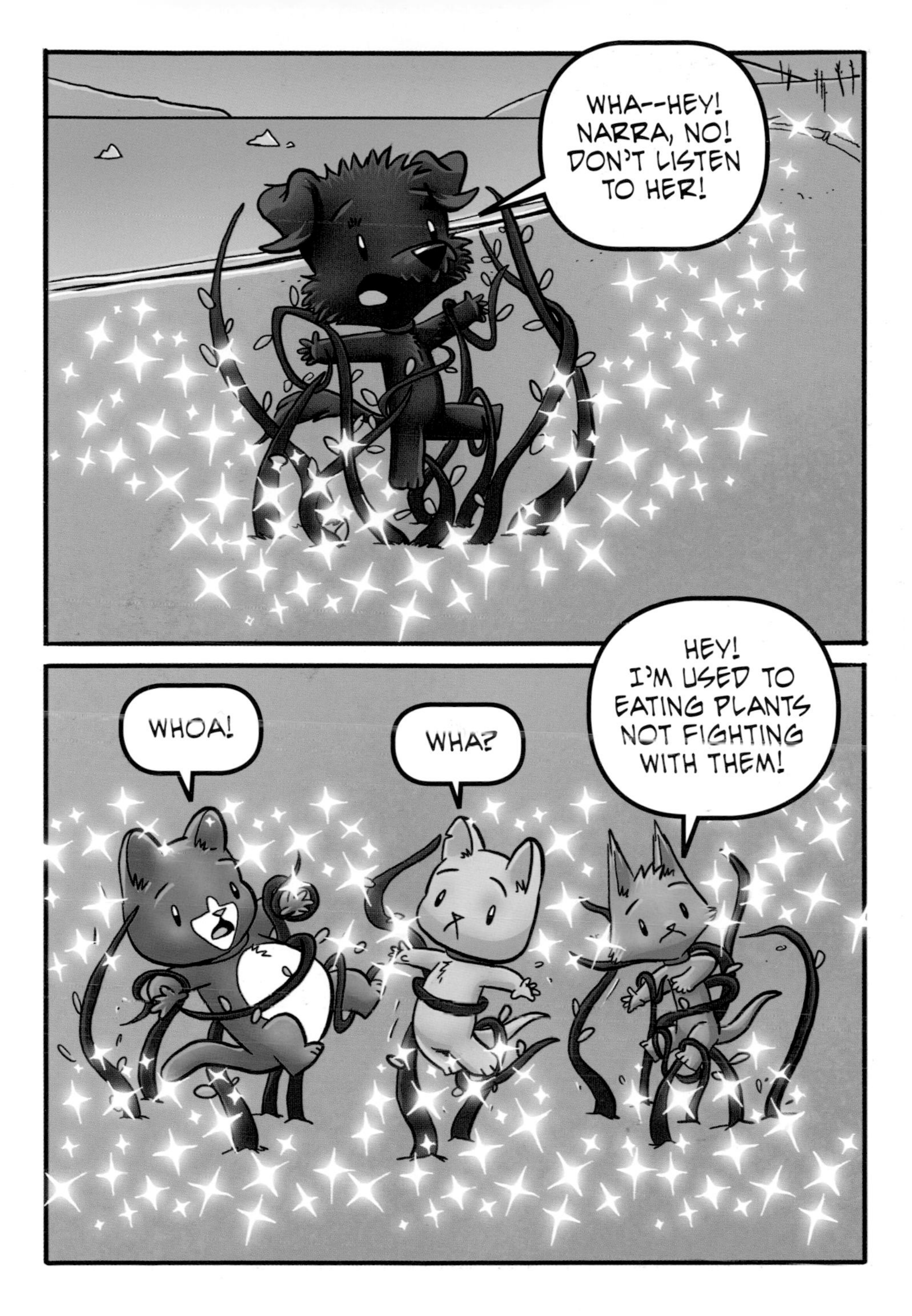
WHA--HEY! NARRA, NO! DON'T LISTEN TO HER!
WHOA!
WHA?
HEY! I'M USED TO EATING PLANTS NOT FIGHTING WITH THEM!

I'M OUTTA HERE!

FWOOOOSH!
CRASH!

OH NO! I CAN'T MOVE!

MELLYBEAN, I'M STUCK-- WHAT CAN WE DO?

HANG ON, I HAVE AN IDEA!

BUTTERNUT, TRY CHEWING THROUGH THE VINES LIKE YOU DO WITH THE TV CABLES BACK HOME!
OKAY!
CHOMP
CHOMP
CHOMP

RETTA, CAN YOU STILL USE YOUR POWERS TO CONTROL THE WATER?
I SEE WHAT YOU'RE THINKING...

YEAH, I THINK I CAN MOVE MY TAIL!

SPLASH THEM WITH WATER!
YEAH, THAT MIGHT BREAK THEIR TRANCE!

HA HA, DRAGONSEAL, YOU'RE MINE NOW!

JUST LOOK AT MY MACHINE...BEST NOT TO FIGHT IT...

I'M FREE! I DID IT!

IT'S POINTLESS TO RESIST!

QUICK, BUTTERNUT, GET THE REST OF US OUT. RETTA IS SUMMONING THE WATER!

UH-OH!

YIKES.

QUICK, GUYS! UP THAT TREE!

ZIP!
ZIP!
ZIP!
ZIP!

TIDAL WAVE!

SPLOOSH!

WAH!
AAAAHH!
EEEK!

SPLOOSH!

CHAPTER 9
AWAKENINGS

NARRA! CATCH HETTY AND LEMMY!

HUH?

GROWL!

OW--
HEY!
FWISH!
RAWR!
RUMBLE
RUMBLE

WHAT DO I DO NOW?

DUNK THEM IN THE WATER!

I CAN'T REACH! LEMMY TRAPPED MY FEET!

RETTA, YOU GOT ONE MORE IN YOU?

YOU BET! ONE MORE TIDAL WAVE COMING RIGHT UP!

SLOSH!

NARRA!
WHAT ARE YOU DOING HERE? AND WHY ARE WE ALL WET?

I DON'T REALLY KNOW. I'M STILL TRYING TO FIGURE THAT OUT MYSELF!

OOOG...

OH NO! IT'S GONE! WHERE DID IT GO?!

LOOKING FOR THESE?

HA HA HA! NOW I'LL HAVE ALL THE POWER--KING OF THE PEOPLE AND THE CREATURES!

SO HOW DOES THIS THING WORK, ANYWAY?

POKE POKE

I SENSE ANOTHER GAME OF KEEP-AWAY COMING UP!

BOOP!
HEY!

IF YOU WANT IT, YOU HAVE TO CATCH ME!

HEY!
GET BACK
HERE!
YEAH! COME BACK
WITH MY MACHINE!

HETTY!
CAN I GET A
LITTLE HELP?

SURE THING,
MELLY!

HEY, NO FAIR.
YEAH, THAT'S CHEATING!

MY LORD, ALLOW ME TO GIVE YOU A BOOST!

HA HA!

ARGH! GIVE... IT... TO... ME!

HEY--I GOT IT. IT'S MINE!

NO, IT'S MINE. I MADE IT!
FINDERS KEEPERS!

LET GO,
LET GO,
LET GO!
NO, *YOU*
LET GO!

I GOT IT, MY LORD!

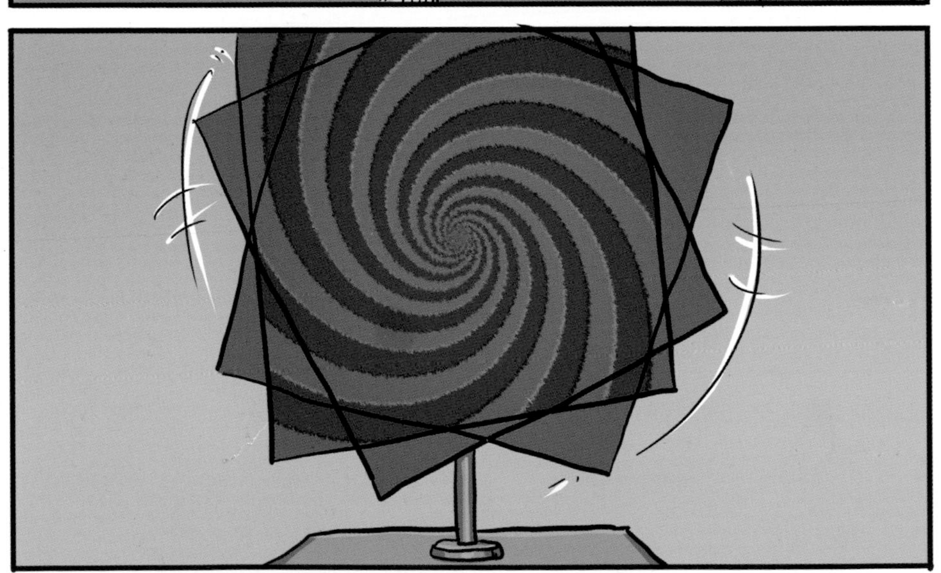

HMMM...

I WONDER...

SIT.

HEY, IT WORKED!
THAT'S A GOOD SIT!

UH, MELLY? WHAT'S GOING ON?

WILMA HYPNOTIZED YOU ALL USING THIS MACHINE!

HYPNOTIZED?

BUT IT'S OKAY NOW. WE CAN MAKE THEM BE GOOD! SEE?

STAY.

OH MY GOSH, RETTA, ARE YOU OKAY? DID I BURY YOU UNDER THOSE ROCKS?
IT'S OKAY. YOU WERE UNDER MIND CONTROL.

IT'S SO NICE TO SEE YOU GUYS AGAIN AFTER ALL THESE YEARS.

I GUESS ONE GOOD THING ABOUT WILMA'S MISCHIEF IS THAT IT FINALLY BROUGHT US ALL BACK TOGETHER.

I DON'T KNOW ABOUT YOU, BUT AFTER THIS, I'M READY TO GO BACK INTO HIDING.

NO, NO, NO...WAIT, DON'T GO. THE REST OF THE HUMANS ARE GOOD. IT'S JUST THESE THREE THAT ARE THE BAD APPLES OF THE BUNCH.

AND THEY'RE BEING GOOD NOW, SEE?

HIGH FIVE!

I BELIEVE THIS BELONGS TO YOU, NARRA!

THANKS, BUT I THINK I HAVE A BETTER IDEA OF WHAT TO DO WITH THIS NOW THAT MY FRIENDS ARE BACK...

GUYS, LET'S ALL GO BACK TO THE KINGDOM. YOU CAN SEE FOR YOURSELF, CREATURES AND HUMANS LIVING IN HARMONY JUST LIKE THE OLD DAYS.
NOW THAT'S SOMETHING I WOULD LOVE TO SEE.
COME ON EVERYBODY! FOLLOW NARRA!

CHAPTER 10
ALL TOGETHER NOW

YOUR HIGHNESS! WELCOME HOME!

GLAD TO BE BACK, MS. COOPER! BUT YOU DON'T HAVE TO CALL ME "YOUR HIGHNESS" ANYMORE.
WHILE I'M THANKFUL TO MELLY AND YOU ALL FOR LETTING ME BE KING, I THINK THE LAND WILL BE BETTER SERVED WITHOUT A KING FROM NOW ON.

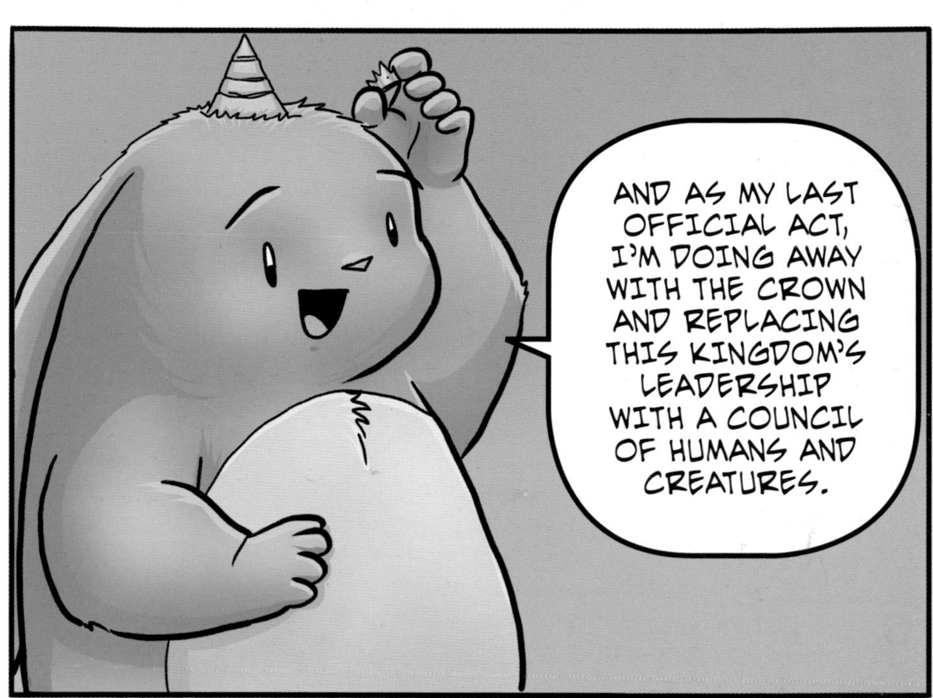
AND AS MY LAST OFFICIAL ACT, I'M DOING AWAY WITH THE CROWN AND REPLACING THIS KINGDOM'S LEADERSHIP WITH A COUNCIL OF HUMANS AND CREATURES.

NO ONE PERSON SHOULD HAVE THE POWER TO RULE. IT'S TOO DANGEROUS AND TOO STRESSFUL. I'VE SEEN WHAT WE CAN DO TOGETHER, SO WHY NOT RULE TOGETHER?

THAT'S A WONDERFUL IDEA, NARRA!

WHAT DO YOU GUYS SAY? WILL YOU BE ON THE COUNCIL WITH US?

WITH NO KING, NO ONE CAN HUNT US, SO I GUESS THAT WOULD BE OKAY.

I DON'T KNOW, NARRA. WE HAD PEACE WITH THE HUMANS ONCE BEFORE, AND THAT DIDN'T WORK OUT SO WELL...

BUT THIS TIME, WE'LL BE WORKING AS A TEAM TO BE GOOD LEADERS FOR THEM.

I GUESS WE CAN GIVE IT A TRY.

WELL, IF I'M NOT GOING TO BE LIVING IN MY CAVE ANYMORE, THE FIRST ITEM OF BUSINESS SHOULD BE TO SPRUCE THIS PLACE UP A BIT...

HETTY, WILL YOU GIVE ME A HAND?
SURE THING, LEMMY!

THE SKY COULD USE SOME ACCENTS.

WOOOOOOOOOW!

AND HOW ABOUT MAKING THE KINGDOM A WATERFRONT PROPERTY? LEMMY, CARE TO HELP OUT?
YES, MA'AM!

MAYBE SOME SPLASHES OF COLOR TO OFFSET ALL THIS GREEN WOULD LOOK NICE?
WHOOOOOOA!

WHAT ABOUT GETTING RID OF THE WALLS AROUND THE CITY SO EVERYONE KNOWS THEY'RE WELCOME?

I THINK HETTY AND I CAN HANDLE THAT!

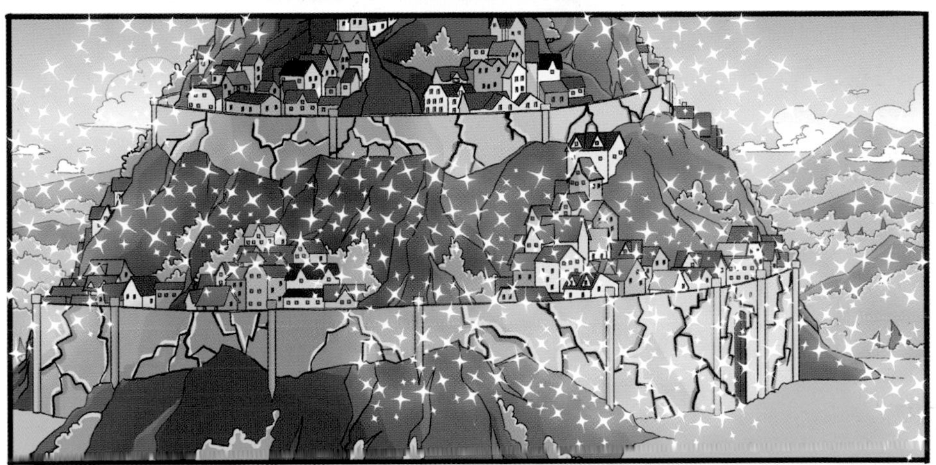

THERE WE GO! THE LAND OF ADO IS STARTING TO LOOK LIKE THE GOOD OLD DAYS AGAIN.

NOT TOO BAD, IF I MAY SAY SO MYSELF!

IT'S SO NICE!
CLAP CLAP CLAP
CLAP CLAP CLAP
CLAP CLAP CLAP

AND IT'S ALL THANKS TO YOU, MELLYBEAN. IF YOU DIDN'T COME ALONG TO SAVE US FROM THE KING, NONE OF THIS WOULD HAVE HAPPENED.
IT WORKED OUT BECAUSE WE ALL DID IT TOGETHER!
ISN'T THAT RIGHT, GUYS?
GUYS?

HMMMM, I THINK I'LL GO FOR SOME CHUNKY TUNA NEXT!
GET SOME FOR US TOO!
THIS SURE IS GREAT--WE HAVE THREE CAN OPENERS NOW!

OH YEAH...MAYBE OUR SECOND ORDER OF BUSINESS SHOULD BE TO UN-HYPNOTIZE OUR TROUBLESOME TRIO?
ONE SPLASH OF COLD WATER, COMING RIGHT UP!

WHILE YOU DO THAT, WE SHOULD PROBABLY GET GOING. MAMA AND PAPA WILL BE COMING HOME FROM WORK SOON AND WE DON'T WANT THEM TO WORRY ABOUT US.

COME, ON GUYS, WE SHOULD BE GETTING HOME.

AW...THINGS WERE JUST STARTING TO GET GOOD!

WHAT ABOUT MAMA AND PAPA? DON'T YOU MISS THEM?

YEAH, YOU'RE RIGHT... AND THEY ARE PRETTY GOOD AT GIVING SKRITCHES.

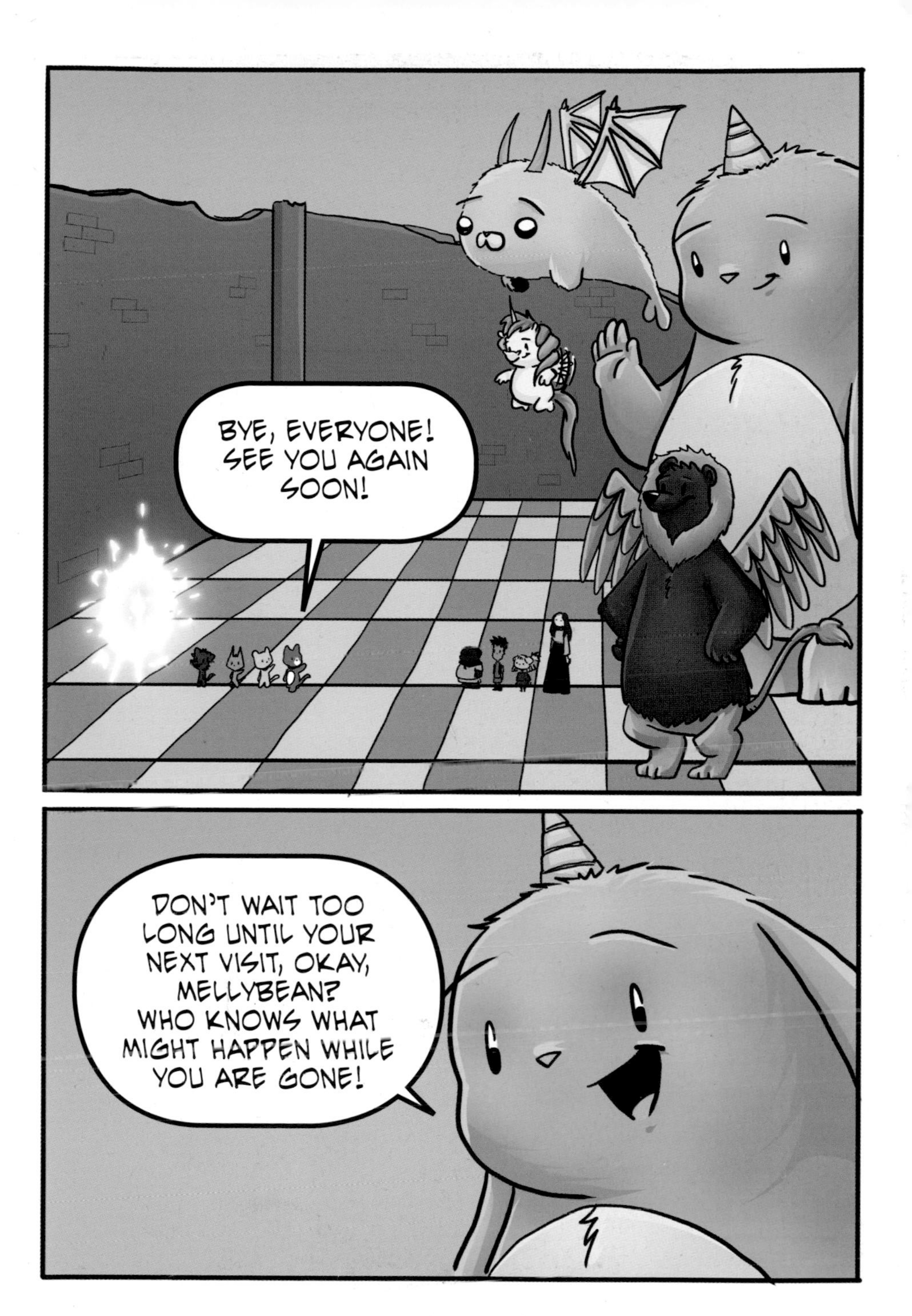
BYE, EVERYONE! SEE YOU AGAIN SOON!
DON'T WAIT TOO LONG UNTIL YOUR NEXT VISIT, OKAY, MELLYBEAN? WHO KNOWS WHAT MIGHT HAPPEN WHILE YOU ARE GONE!

HEY, MAYBE YOU CAN VISIT US NEXT TIME!
NOW THAT SOUNDS LIKE AN ADVENTURE!

CHAPTER 11
HOME SWEET HOME

SHOOP!

PLOP!
SHOOP!
SHOOP!

PLOP!
SHOOP!

PLOP!

CLICK
CLACK

EVERYBODY INSIDE, HURRY! MAMA AND PAPA ARE HOME!

HI, GUYS!
AW...HAVE YOU BEEN WAITING FOR US THIS WHOLE TIME?

MEOW.
BARK!
MEW.
MAOW.

AW, WE MISSED YOU TOO!

PEANUT BUTTER MELLY SANDWICH!

NOW, WHO'S READY FOR CHEESEBURGERS AND CHICKEN NUGGETS?!

HEY, WHAT'S THAT BIG HOLE IN THE BACKYARD?

DID YOU FORGET TO COVER UP THE HOLE WITH THE BLANKET AGAIN?

I THOUGHT YOU WERE GOING TO DO THAT.

HM, MUST BE THOSE PESKY SKUNKS AGAIN. MAYBE I'LL GO TAKE A LOOK AFTER DINNER.

EXTRA-SPECIAL THANKS!

It has been a dream come true making these books about Mellybean. I'd just like to take a moment to thank everyone who has helped along the way.

Carol Hou and the Hou family for their unconditional love and support,

my agent, Gemma Cooper, for believing in the series,

my editor, Chris Hernandez, for taking a chance on us,

my designer, Jessica Jenkins, for her great work on the book,

my publicist, Jennifer Dee, for spreading the word,

my colorist, Valery Kutz, for her hard work and great job coloring the series,

Jeff and Nurgul Tseng for their emotional support,

Jared and Wall-E Kim for letting me live at their house while making this book,

Wyatt, Emi, and Gwenny for being great test readers,

Ali and Murti of Streamlabs for their dog-friendly offices,

Kevin and Andrea Tseng Rioux for introducing me to their network,

Amy Rubin, Sandi Dennis, and Nan Brown for hosting my author visits with their students,

All of my virtual author visit hosts,

Beyond the Trope and *Hey! I Gotta New Book* podcasts for having me on their shows,

the Milo Foundation, where we got Melly,

Book Passage and Books Inc. for working with me to promote Mellybean,

all the booksellers who brought Mellybean into their store,

all of you who read the books,

and Mellybean for inspiring it all.

MAKING A GRAPHIC NOVEL

For those of you who are interested in how the Mellybean books were made—or even making your own graphic novel—here's a quick behind-the-scenes look at how I work!

STEP 1 is to write out the script. I do this for the whole book before drawing anything.

For each page, I write what goes on and what the characters say. The bullet points indicate a new panel, so I know how many to draw on each page.

Let's take a look at pages 13 and 14 for the next steps…

CHAPTER 2: Keep Away

Page 10

- Meanwhile, at the top of the mountain kingdom…
- Mellybean stares at Butternut and Chuck eating their food.
- Butternut and Chuck just ignore her.
- Mellybean: "Whimper"

Page 11

- Chuck: "Your stare only makes humans give you their food, Mellybean"
- Butternut: "Besides, you know you're not supposed to eat cat food."
- Melly: "But...but..."
- Melly: "Have you noticed that I haven't barked at you for eating wires, scratching the sofa, and being on the counter?"

Page 12

- Butternut: "That's because everything here is made of wood and stone... there are no wires or sofas!"
- Melly: "But you noticed right? I'm being good, that means you should share your food with me."
- Chuck: "Not a chance, Melly."
- Melly: "Aw, come on…"

Page 13

- Melly paws at an unopened can of food in front of them.
- Butternut: "Hey, don't play with that - it's our last can until Tugs gets back with another haul."
- Melly perks up.

Page 14

- Melly: "So...you want this?"
- Butternut: "Yes, give it here."
- Melly: "Oh boy! A game of keep away!"
- Melly turns and runs with the can in her mouth "You have to catch me!"

STEP 2 is to sketch out the scene using a pencil.

I use a blue one so that after I ink the artwork, only my black inked lines show up when I scan a page into my computer.

This stage is like a rough draft. The drawings can be a bit scribbley here because I'll refine all of the messy lines when I go to add inks.

STEP 3 is to ink the line-work. I trace over the rough drawings using a brushpen or black marker so that there are solid lines.

This is basically like making a coloring book. Now the art can be colored inside of those clean lines.

STEP 4 is to add color and the dialogue.

My friend Valery uses a computer program called Photoshop to color the pages.

Then I add in the word balloons, also using the computer because fonts are nicer than my handwriting.

Once all the pages are drawn and lettered, they go off to a printer to be made into a book.

AND THAT'S HOW THE MELLYBEAN GRAPHIC NOVELS ARE MADE!